Which Way, Black Cat?

(hardcover title: Proudfoot's Way)

by ELEANOR FRANCES LATTIMORE

illustrated by Beatrice Darwin

SCHOLASTIC BOOK SERVICES
New York Toronto London Sydney Auckland Tokyo

ISBN 0-590-30040-7

This edition is published by Scholastic Book Services, a division of Scholastic Magazines, Inc., 50 West 44th Street, New York, New York 10036, by arrangement with William Morrow and Company, Inc., publishers of the book under the title PROUDFOOT'S WAY.

12 11 10 9 8 7 6 5 4 3 2 1 9 9/7 0 1 2 3 4/8
Printed in the U.S.A.

Contents

Phoebe and Mrs. Morse

Phoebe did not like Mrs. Morse. She had kept house for the Tuckers ever since Phoebe's mother had died, and Phoebe's father called her "a good old soul," but Phoebe still didn't like her. True, she had taken good care of Phoebe and her brother, Tom, seeing that they got off to school in the morning and looking after their clothes, but she was never someone they felt like confiding in. And they couldn't help exchanging secret smiles when they heard her praising them sky-high to their father.

Phoebe heard no words of praise now that her father and Tom had gone away. Mrs. Morse grew fussier and crabbier every day. She was always saying, "Carry out the garbage, Phoebe," or "Go and dust the sitting room," which made Phoebe feel like Cinderella. Mrs. Morse didn't seem to think that a nine-year-old girl should ever have time for fun.

"I wish that Daddy hadn't left me behind," Phoebe said to herself. The old farmhouse that was her home no longer felt homelike on account of Mrs. Morse's endless dusting and sweeping. Phoebe was sure that

Mrs. Morse would die without her broom!

Phoebe had brown eyes and curly hair that was shorter than Tom's. Like many boys of his age, which was thirteen, Tom had let his hair grow to almost shoulder length. But Phoebe's hair got curlier the longer it grew, and Mrs. Morse snipped off the curls with her sharp shears. "You look better now. Not so wild," Mrs. Morse told her. Phoebe looked at herself in the hall mirror. She wasn't pleased with her looks. If only she had long, straight, golden hair like a fairy-tale princess!

Phoebe had read any number of books by the time she was nine. She had read about princesses and Gypsies and witches. . . . When she was a little girl, really little, she had snuggled up on her mother's lap while her mother read to her. Their favorite reading chair was in the sitting room, not the parlor, where the chairs were stiff and uncomfortable. The parlor was seldom used. But it was Mrs. Morse's pride. Once a week she swept, polished, and scrubbed it, as if it had to be kept ready for some visiting king.

Phoebe could not remember clearly what her mother looked like, but she remembered her gentle ways. Once when Mrs. Morse spoke to her sharply she said, "You are not my mother, and I don't have to do what you say," which made Mrs. Morse's black eyes snap with anger.

The house where Phoebe lived was in the southernmost corner of New Hampshire. Her grandfather and his father before him had been farmers, but Phoebe's father was a doctor. Dr. Tucker had practiced in the nearby town of Linton until, early in the summer, he had a chance to take over a larger practice in the city of Greenfield.

"That's down in Massachusetts, but it's not really far away," her father said to Phoebe.

Phoebe nodded. There was a map on the wall of her school classroom that showed all of the New England states. New Hampshire and Vermont were side-by-side, like twins, and right below them was Massachusetts, which was colored pink on the map.

Of course, Phoebe thought that she was going to Greenfield with her father. She couldn't believe her ears when he said that although he was taking Tom with him, he would leave Phoebe, for the present, with Mrs. Morse.

"Why, Daddy?" she asked him.

He drew her onto his knee and said, "I think you'll be better off here during the summer, Phoebe. Your friends are here, and Mrs. Morse is going to stay with you until I can have you with me."

"I'd rather be with you *now*," said Phoebe.

Her father explained that with his new practice he wouldn't have much time to spend with her. "And you need someone to take care of you in the summer, when there's no school," he said.

"I can take care of myself," said Phoebe.

"You're only nine," said her father.

"Well, then, Tom can take care of me," said Phoebe.

"Tom's got to work this summer," her father told her. "He's ready for Grover Academy, all except for his math, and I've arranged for him to go to a tutoring school."

"Tom isn't dumb," put in Phoebe.

"He's far from dumb, though he's behind in math. He wants to get a part-time job to help pay for his tutoring," said her father. "You must be a happy girl, Phoebe, and have a good time with your friends. Write to me if you feel sad, or better still phone me."

He wrote his Greenfield address and phone number on a sheet of paper and said, "Now, Phoebe, let's see a smile."

Phoebe tried to smile, but she couldn't help feeling sad at being left behind....

The friends Phoebe's father had spoken of were the Witherspoon children: Martha, Joel, and Ellen. The Witherspoon family were the Tuckers' nearest neighbors. Mr. Witherspoon was a farmer and rented land from Dr. Tucker. His wife was a shy, delicate person, who seldom left her home. The three young Witherspoons were not only Phoebe's playmates, they were her schoolmates as well. The Tucker and Witherspoon children had gone to school in Linton together, riding back and forth on a bus.

Martha, Joel, and Ellen kept Phoebe from feeling lonely through the months of June and July. They played games, indoors and outdoors, after their chores were done, meeting at the Witherspoons' house instead of the Tuckers' on account of Mrs. Morse's fussiness. But in August the Witherspoon children went to visit their grandparents in Vermont. Phoebe was alone day after day with Mrs. Morse. She felt sad, but not quite sad enough to write or phone her father.

"If only Proudfoot were here!" she said to herself.

Proudfoot was Tom's cat, and Tom had taken him to Greenfield. Phoebe was sure she loved Proudfoot quite as much as Tom did. The thought of his being shut inside a basket for the drive to Greenfield had almost broken her heart. She had whispered words of endearment to him through the holes in the basket. "I bet he hates being cooped up there," she had said to Tom.

"It won't be for long," Tom had replied. "I'm going to let him out as soon as we get to Greenfield. He'll be company for me when I'm doing all that studying. You're lucky, Phoebe. You can stay here in the country, while I work, work, work all summer."

"You'll be with Daddy," said Phoebe.

"He's going to be too busy to spend much time with me," said Tom.

Tom was the one who had found Proudfoot. He had appeared like magic on a Halloween night when the moon was as round and as orange as a pumpkin. His shadow merged with Tom's shadow on the path to the barn, and Tom called out, "Dad! Phoebe! I've found a cat!"

He was a beautiful cat. His coat was as black as soot and as smooth as silk.

Tom had found him, so Proudfoot was Tom's cat. But Phoebe gave him his name. After Tom had let him inside the house on that long-ago Halloween, Phoebe said, "See how proudly he walks!" The name Proudfoot came into her mind right afterward.

"Let's call him Proudfoot," she said to Tom.

"Okay," said Tom. "That suits him."

One pleasant August evening Phoebe was thinking of Proudfoot. She was sitting on the back steps, looking toward the barn and wishing she could see his familiar black shape on the path.

"Where are you, Phoebe?" Mrs. Morse's voice had a sharp edge, like a saw.

"I'm here," Phoebe answered.

"Dawdling," said Mrs. Morse, coming to the back door. "If you haven't anything better to do you can go in and tidy the sitting room."

"Why?" asked Phoebe.

"I told you, but you've forgotten, that my friends are coming to spend the evening with me," said Mrs.

Morse. "That room looks a sight. Your toys and books are all over the place." She added under her breath, "Such a troublesome girl."

"Those aren't *toys*," said Phoebe. What Mrs. Morse had referred to was the deck of cards with which she had been building a castle. Her father's new address was 10 Castle Road, Greenfield, which led Phoebe to imagine a sort of Disneyland castle. She had tried to draw a castle and to build one. "I'll put away my things," she said, and went into the house. She didn't want Mrs. Morse's friends to see what she had been making.

Phoebe didn't care for these friends of Mrs. Morse, who had begun to come to the house after her father and Tom had left. There were three of them, and Phoebe thought they were like three witches. Their names were Mrs. Black, Mrs. Weed, and Mrs. Stone. They lived on the Linton road in an old house that was not as fine as the Tuckers'. It was a treat for them to visit her, Mrs. Morse told Phoebe. She served them cold lemonade and hot doughnuts in the sitting room, which was their meeting place. Did they pay any attention to Phoebe? None at all, except to remark on how fast she was growing. "Like a weed," they said.

Phoebe usually fled to her room when she heard them coming.

"You can take a book upstairs with you, and I'll

bring you up some doughnuts later," Mrs. Morse said to Phoebe.

Phoebe touched her card castle with one finger, and it collapsed. She put all the cards back in their case and the books back on the shelves. All but one. The book she carried up to her room was one that Tom had finished reading and left behind. Phoebe liked Tom's books better than her own. For one thing, they were more exciting.

Phoebe and Proudfoot

Phoebe's bedroom was above the kitchen. From its window she had a view of the barn and the pasture-land beyond. Right after Phoebe heard Mrs. Morse greeting her friends she laid down Tom's book and looked out the window. The evening star showed in the sky. As Phoebe was starting to make a wish on the star she saw a shadow move along the path from the barn.

What was that? A dog or a fox?

It was a cat-shaped shadow.

Phoebe had been thinking of Proudfoot and wishing that she could see him. But Tom had taken Proudfoot to Greenfield. "That can't be Proudfoot," Phoebe said to herself.

She stood close to the window, listening. . . . The shadow had disappeared, but Phoebe heard a scratching sound at the back door.

That *is* Proudfoot, thought Phoebe. She raced down the stairs, opened the back door, and there — sure enough — was the cat. He looked thinner, but he was the same proud cat. He was too proud to mew, but when Phoebe lifted him up in her arms, he began to purr. Proudfoot's purr was a low, rumbling sound, like distant thunder.

Phoebe was still hugging and patting Proudfoot when Mrs. Morse came sailing into the kitchen.

"So he came back. I thought he would," said Mrs. Morse. She opened the oven door and put some doughnuts in to heat.

"How did he know the way? When he left home he was in a basket, inside Daddy's car," said Phoebe.

Mrs. Morse smiled. When she smiled, her nose and chin almost met. "Cats can always find their way home," she said. "You run upstairs now, Phoebe. I'll give the cat something to eat as soon as I have the refreshments ready for my friends."

"I can feed him," said Phoebe.

"No, you go on upstairs. Bedtime," said Mrs. Morse.

Phoebe hated to be ordered around by Mrs. Morse. It was *not* her bedtime yet. She often stayed up much later. But she was too young to win an argument with Mrs. Morse, who was years and years older.

She went back upstairs, knowing that Mrs. Morse would give Proudfoot a hearty meal. Mrs. Morse had always been partial to him. He was a good mouser, and there were mice in the barn, where Mr. Witherspoon stored hay.

Anyway, I'm glad I don't have to see Mrs. Morse's

friends, thought Phoebe. All three of the women were thin; all of them wore black or gray. They never smiled, and when they laughed they sounded like hens cackling.

It was dark now in Phoebe's room. She turned on the light and got ready for bed. If Tom were at home, she could have watched a TV show with him on the small portable set he had been given for Christmas.

I could read some more of Tom's book, thought Phoebe. But she didn't feel like reading now. She felt too excited by Proudfoot's unexpected return.

Mrs. Morse came into her room, carrying a tray on which were a jelly glass of lemonade and two piping hot doughnuts. "Here you are," she said.

Phoebe thanked her with a smile. Proudfoot was home, and for the present she was happy, as her father wished her to be.

The next morning Phoebe was up long before breakfast time. She wanted to make sure that Proudfoot had stayed on the farm. Proudfoot's favorite night place had always been the barn. Phoebe walked toward the barn, calling his name, and Proudfoot came to meet her. She noticed how carefully he stepped through the dewy grass.

"Oh, Proudfoot, you were clever to find your way home," said Phoebe.

Proudfoot arched his back and waved the tip of his tail. Though he could not speak, he had ways of replying to a compliment.

Phoebe's thoughts turned to Tom. She was sure he must be worried by the disappearance of his Halloween cat! I'll call him up and tell him that Proudfoot's safe, she thought.

She went back to the house and found the sheet of paper on which her father had written his telephone number. The phone was in the hallway between the sitting room and the kitchen. It was a wall phone and high for Phoebe to reach, but she moved a chair over and stood on it.

"*Phoebe!*"

Phoebe nearly fell off the chair.

"What are you doing, Phoebe?"

"Phoning Tom," said Phoebe.

Mrs. Morse swept her off the chair, saying, "Long-distance calls are a sheer waste of money."

"But I want to tell Tom that Proudfoot's here," protested Phoebe.

"He'll know soon enough, when I send my weekly report to your father," said Mrs. Morse.

Phoebe hadn't heard anything about a weekly report before. Tears of vexation filled her eyes at being stopped from phoning. How can Mrs. Morse be so mean? she wondered.

"You've nothing to cry about. You don't know how lucky you are to live in this fine house," said Mrs. Morse.

All Mrs. Morse seemed to care about was the farmhouse — which wasn't even her own.

Proudfoot was in and out of the house during the next few days. He had always been a restless cat, but he was more restless now than Phoebe had ever seen him. He jumped up on Phoebe's lap when she was shelling peas, causing her to spill a whole panful. Another time he jumped on Mrs. Morse's lap and got entangled in some stockings she was darning.

"I expect he's looking for Tom," said Phoebe.

"He knows better than that. He knows quite well where Tom is," said Mrs. Morse.

"He must know he belongs to Tom," said Phoebe.

Mrs. Morse sniffed. "Cats belong only to themselves," she said, shaking her broom.

Phoebe looked at Proudfoot. He blinked his eyes at her. They were topaz eyes, Tom had told Phoebe. She remembered that, as she remembered many things he had told her.

Mrs. Morse spoke again. "Do you know what ails this cat, Phoebe? He likes you, but he likes me too, and he's trying to decide who he likes best."

"He likes me best," said Phoebe quickly.

"Don't be too sure," said Mrs. Morse. "I think I understand cats better than you do."

Phoebe didn't want to listen to her any longer. She went off to the barn to think things over.

The Tuckers' barn was painted a cheerful red. When Tom was at home, Phoebe had loved to go there to watch him milk the cows, Buttercup and

Daisy. Milking the cows had been one of Tom's chores. Proudfoot followed him to the barn both morning and evening and waited patiently while Tom milked. Proudfoot knew his turn would come for some fresh milk, which he daintily lapped from an old pie tin. Since June, Mr. Witherspoon had taken care of the cows. He was a stern-looking man, but friendly toward Tom and Phoebe because his children thought so much of them.

Ellen, the youngest Witherspoon, was one day older than Phoebe, which made them special friends. Ellen had sent Phoebe a postcard from her grandparents' home in Vermont. On it she had written, "I wish you were here." The postmark on the card said *Brattleboro, Vt.* Phoebe had never been there.

She kept the card in a box with two letters from her father. Mrs. Morse usually pounced on the mail, but once in a while Phoebe got to the mail first.

She frowned as she thought how it hadn't done a bit of good to get to the telephone first.

Good-bye to the Farm

One week after Proudfoot's return, Mrs. Morse's friends came again. Not much had happened during the week. The Witherspoon children were still away, and Proudfoot, although acting restless, was still at the farm. Often Phoebe, watching him, wondered if Mrs. Morse was right in thinking he was trying to decide who he liked best.

How does she know so much about cats? Phoebe wondered.

She saw Mrs. Morse's friends arriving in their old car, which bounced along the dirt road. She was out in the yard with Proudfoot. The supper dishes were washed and dried, and Mrs. Morse was in the kitchen, squeezing lemons for lemonade.

It was a beautiful evening. Fireflies darted hither and thither, and Phoebe and Proudfoot were both darting after them. The car jolted to a stop a few feet away, and Mrs. Black, Mrs. Stone, and Mrs. Weed stepped out.

They all three spoke at once. "Good evening, Phoebe!"

"Good evening," Phoebe answered. But she didn't offer to shake hands with them. They were too witchy.

"And here is your dear cat," said Mrs. Weed. She put out a hand to pat Proudfoot, and he did not turn away. He let himself be petted; he even purred.

Phoebe felt quite provoked with him.

When Mrs. Morse came out of the house to greet her friends, Proudfoot turned his back on all four women and went off to the barn. Phoebe didn't feel like going to her room just yet. Instead, she went to the barn to see what Proudfoot was up to.

The cows were in their stalls, peacefully chewing their cuds. The barn had a summery smell, a mixture of cows and sweet hay. There may have been a mouse smell too, because Phoebe saw Proudfoot crouching. Ugh, she thought; she would not care to eat a raw mouse.

The barn was wired for electricity, but Phoebe didn't turn on the light. She liked the twilight dimness of the barn. She settled herself on a milking stool, taking care not to let the hem of her dress touch the floor. First her mother, then Mrs. Morse, had taught Phoebe to be neat.

Through the open door Phoebe could see the moon, which was almost full but a bit lopsided. It made her think of a tippy boat. There was a lot about boats in the book Tom had left behind. The hero of the story had run away to sea and had all kinds of adventures. Phoebe wished something exciting would happen to her!

The telephone was ringing in the house. The back door had been left open, and Phoebe heard the ringing plainly. Her first thought was, That's Daddy! She jumped up from the milking stool and ran toward the house as fast as she could. In her hurry, she stubbed her toe against some unseen object: a pebble or stone hidden in the grass. The phone had stopped ringing by the time Phoebe reached the house.

Had Mrs. Morse answered the call? And was it Daddy? Phoebe wondered.

Mrs. Morse was frugal with lights, so the house was dark except for the sitting room, from which a streak of light shone into the hall through the partly open door. As Phoebe stood beside the phone she heard Mrs. Morse's voice, and although she knew it wasn't right to eavesdrop, she couldn't help listening.

"I told him that Phoebe had gone to bed," Mrs. Morse said. "Why should we interrupt our visit to chase after a child?"

"It *was* Daddy who called up," Phoebe said to herself. She stood perfectly still. She was sure that no one knew she was there in the hall.

"When is he coming for her?" Was that Mrs. Weed speaking?

"Perhaps he won't come," said Mrs. Morse. "He knows that Phoebe is well taken care of here and that she's best off where she is. I hope he does leave her with me. This house seems like my own after I've kept it pretty and tidy all these years."

"But he won't leave her here forever," said another voice, which might have been Mrs. Black's.

"Who knows? I'm sure Dr. Tucker doesn't want her around, and I'm going to tell her so," said Mrs. Morse.

I don't believe *that*, thought Phoebe, who had been growing more shocked the longer she listened. She knew that her father loved her. She was sure that he wanted her.

One of the women laughed like a cackling hen.

Phoebe didn't want to listen any longer. With her mind in a whirl she went softly through the kitchen and back to the barn where she had left Proudfoot. Mrs. Morse was meaner than she had ever supposed, and Phoebe longed for the comfort of her father's arms.

"I don't know what to do!" she said to herself. Then a very daring idea came into Phoebe's head. *She would run away from the farm and, somehow, get to her father and Tom in Greenfield.*

Phoebe didn't know how to get to Greenfield. "But Proudfoot knows the way," she said to herself. With Proudfoot as her guide she would not be afraid to travel miles and miles. . . .

When should she leave? Phoebe decided to leave that very night.

Proudfoot was an intelligent cat, as all the family

knew. To Phoebe, he seemed a mixture of Puss-in-Boots and Dick Whittington's famous cat. If I can make Proudfoot understand, he will show me the way, thought Phoebe. She called to him softly, "Come here, Proudfoot."

Proudfoot came close enough for Phoebe to pat him, and she asked him, "Do you like Tom and me best, Proudfoot?"

He looked up into her face with his topaz eyes and purred in reply.

"Will you show me the way to Greenfield? We'll see Tom there," said Phoebe.

Proudfoot kept on purring.

Phoebe whispered in his ear, "Wait here while I pack some things." Quietly, on tiptoes, she went back inside the house.

Once safely in her own room, Phoebe pulled open a bureau drawer. Her father had given her three dollars before he went away, and he had sent her a five-dollar bill in one of the two letters she had received from him. "Buy yourself something pretty in Linton," he had told her, but Phoebe hadn't gone to Linton since the Witherspoon children had left to visit their grandparents. Phoebe didn't like to shop by herself, and she didn't enjoy shopping with Mrs. Morse one bit.

Phoebe took her money out of her bureau drawer and put it in her school satchel, which she planned to take with her instead of a pocketbook. Next, she went into the bathroom to get her toothbrush. Back in her room again, Phoebe folded her pajamas and put them, with her toothbrush, in her satchel. There was no room for a fresh dress, but Phoebe was sure that her father would buy her new, pretty clothes in Greenfield.

Of course, there was no use in trying to phone her father, with Mrs. Morse so close to the telephone. I will just surprise Daddy and Tom, thought Phoebe. Though she knew their address — which would soon be *her* address — by heart, she slipped both of her father's letters into her satchel. His stationery had his phone number printed on it as well as the words *10 Castle Road, Greenfield, Mass.*

Phoebe's most precious possession and the only thing she had of value was a little gold locket. It was shaped like a heart and inside the heart was a tiny, blurred snapshot of her mother. Phoebe didn't pack the locket, because she wore it day and night on a chain around her neck. The chain was of gold too.

I'm ready to leave now, thought Phoebe, picking up her satchel. She went softly down the stairs and out through the kitchen door. Proudfoot was waiting for her in the shadow of the barn. As if he knew the importance of the job she had given him, he trotted ahead of her, tail up.

Off they went together!

To anyone who might have observed them, they

were a strange pair: the curly-haired girl following in the footsteps of the black cat. The brown-and-white dress of checked gingham that Phoebe wore, like all of her clothes, had been bought by Mrs. Morse. The brown looked black in the moonlight. Phoebe's shoes were brown oxfords — sensible shoes. The school satchel, slung over her shoulder, bumped against her side as she stumbled across a rough, stony pasture.

For Proudfoot wasn't taking the road to Linton. Not he. He led Phoebe across three pastures before they entered some woods. Cats hate traffic, and even at night there were apt to be trucks or joyriders on the Linton road, so Proudfoot kept away from it.

Phoebe had explored these woods in the daytime with Tom, but she hadn't known that they were on the way to Greenfield. Still, Proudfoot must know, she thought. So she followed him along a queer little path that he seemed familiar with.

He never stopped walking. But he turned his head now and then as if to make sure that Phoebe was still behind him.

Moonlight filtered down through the trees. Most of the trees were pines, but some whitebarked birch trees gleamed as pale as ghosts. Phoebe was glad that she had a cat for company: a cat with claws, a cat with sharp, little teeth. Best of all, a cat who knew his way through the night woods.

The Haunted House

The tippy moon was in a different part of the sky by the time Phoebe and Proudfoot came out of the woods. A quiet, untraveled sort of road lay before them, and Phoebe said aloud, "It's the River Road."

The old River Road hadn't been much used since a new highway was built on higher ground, but Phoebe had picnicked near there with her father and Tom. "The Connecticut River is close by," she said. "It separates New Hampshire from Vermont."

Phoebe was speaking to Proudfoot. But if he heard her, he paid no attention. He kept trotting ahead. Cats are usually at their most active in the night, and this intelligent black cat hadn't slowed up once.

Phoebe, on the other hand, was so tired that she felt she could lie down anywhere and go to sleep. However, she didn't dare to lose sight of Proudfoot. What would she do without him?

Proudfoot's black shape disappeared around a bend in the road, and Phoebe, following, saw a house looming large and white in the moonlight. Two firs that looked like untrimmed Christmas trees grew as tall as the rooftop on either side of the house. Proudfoot walked unhesitatingly to the front door and sat down on the steps.

He's tired too, thought Phoebe.

The house had a deserted look. No lights showed inside, and when Phoebe knocked, a bit timidly, no one answered her knock.

Proudfoot raised a paw and scratched against the door.

He wants me to open it for him, thought Phoebe. She turned the knob. The door opened, and Phoebe peeked inside. The house appeared to have been vacant for a long time.

Proudfoot stalked ahead of Phoebe into a big room that was lighted only by the moon outside. Phoebe followed, thinking, We can sleep here. It smelled musty inside the house, so she left the door open.

The room had no furniture in it except for a sofa and a footstool. While Proudfoot jumped on the stool and began to wash himself, Phoebe lay down on the sofa. There were holes in it from which the stuffing protruded, and there was no pillow, but Phoebe was so tired that she felt ready to sleep and sleep.

When she rolled over on her school satchel she laid it on the floor. Then she took off her shoes. "Good night, Proudfoot," she said. In a minute she was fast asleep.

But what frightening dreams Phoebe had that

night! Her dreams were of ghosts and goblins and witches. They had no faces and they made no noise, but they circled around her sofa and wouldn't let her escape from them. Finally she woke up, trembling.

The room was dark, because the moon no longer shone through the windows. She must be in the Haunted House, thought Phoebe, remembering that Tom had told her about a haunted house on the River Road.

"The house wasn't always haunted," Tom had said. "In fact, it wasn't actually a house. It was an inn. Stagecoaches stopped there in the olden days." Tom liked to repeat stories he had heard about the olden days long before he and Phoebe were born.

"Then what happened?" Phoebe had asked.

"The inn went through bad times. Someone died there, and people say he was murdered," said Tom.

Remembering that story, Phoebe sat bolt upright on the sofa. There's probably at least one real ghost here right now, she thought.

Proudfoot came over to the sofa and leaped up beside Phoebe. He moved his feet restlessly, and at first she thought that he was "digging potatoes." But he would not settle down, and this cat who never mewed opened his mouth to make small, anxious sounds.

"What's the matter, Proudfoot? Did you have bad dreams too?" asked Phoebe.

Proudfoot did not purr a reply.

Phoebe stroked his smooth head and his glossy back. "Please settle down so I can go back to sleep," she said.

She lay down again, and Proudfoot turned round and round before perching uneasily just beyond Phoebe's toes.

The next time Phoebe woke up it was broad daylight. A little mouse jumped out from one of the holes in her sofa bed and skittered across the floor. Phoebe was not alarmed. Proudfoot will catch it, she thought. The mouse disappeared under a rotting floorboard. Phoebe looked all around the room.

Where was Proudfoot?

The door was open, as Phoebe had left it the night before. "He's just gone outside," she said to herself, and put on her shoes. The outdoors was as morning-fresh as the house was dismal, and Phoebe, going out to call Proudfoot, felt happy. She was eager to set forth again on the way to Greenfield.

"Proudfoot!" she called.

He did not appear.

"Proudfoot, Proudfoot!" Phoebe kept calling. She walked all around the house, but nowhere did she see any sight of Proudfoot. He couldn't have left me here all by myself, thought Phoebe. Surely he'll be back in a little while!

Beyond a cluster of outbuildings, Phoebe discovered a spring with clear running water. Being thirsty, she made a cup of her hands and drank. Then she splashed some of the cold water on her face. I had better brush my teeth, she thought. So she went back to the house, fetched her toothbrush from her school satchel, and returned to the spring.

She did not see Proudfoot either going or coming.

Brushing her teeth made Phoebe feel cleaner and fresher, but there was a queer feeling in the middle of her stomach. It was partly due to her growing worry about the missing cat and partly due to hunger. She hadn't had anything to eat since supper the night before, a supper Mrs. Morse had cooked at the farm.

Luckily for Phoebe, she was a country-reared child and knew where to look for berries. Blueberries are ripe in August and can often be found in sheltered, sunny spots. Phoebe found some bushes weighted with berries growing beside an old stone wall near the Haunted House. She ate a lot of them, and they tasted delicious. But Phoebe couldn't get over her queer feeling. Where *was* Proudfoot? she wondered. Had he gone back to the farm? Had he left her here alone because he liked Mrs. Morse best?

When those thoughts came into Phoebe's mind they would not go away, and she was so sad that she couldn't help crying. Shaken by sobs, she flung herself down on the grass. She had never expected Proudfoot to desert her.

At last Phoebe sat up. She dried her eyes with the hem of her dress, not having brought a handkerchief. Proudfoot was trying to tell me he was going back to the farm when he wouldn't settle down last night, she thought. He was trying to tell me! Just the same, *I'm* not going back to Mrs. Morse.

Then and there Phoebe made up her mind to go on toward Greenfield by herself — even if she didn't know the way.

Once Phoebe had decided, she felt a little better. She went back inside the house for her school satchel and hurried out again, closing the door behind her. She knew the road to Greenfield would be long for her, but she was glad to be leaving the Haunted House.

The Station-Wagon Family

Phoebe knew some geography. She knew that the Connecticut River flowed south to Massachusetts and on to Connecticut. If she stayed close to the river, she could use it instead of Proudfoot for her guide.

Phoebe's face was set toward the south. She walked along the River Road, humming a tune from one of Tom's favorite records. Before she was half-way through the tune she saw a boy coming toward her on a bicycle. Phoebe jumped out of his way. The boy didn't stop, although he stared at Phoebe. He was wondering, perhaps, where she was going all by herself. Phoebe felt relieved when he had passed by. She didn't want to be questioned, for most people would think she should not go so far alone.

Phoebe walked along quite smartly in her brown oxfords, but after a while she stopped to rest and to admire the wild flowers that grew beside the road. They were so pretty that she picked a nice-sized bunch, although she knew that, like all wild flowers, they would soon fade.

When Phoebe walked on again she played a game of Let's Pretend. She was pretending that she was a bridesmaid. Once, with the Witherspoon girls, she had been to a wedding, and she had never forgotten the lovely dresses of the bridesmaids. Holding her bouquet carefully, Phoebe stepped in time to imaginary organ music.

A car passed by without stopping.

Phoebe walked on and on. At one point the road ran right beside the Connecticut River. Phoebe paused to look down at the water, which reflected sky and trees. Looking up, she saw white summer clouds piled one on top of another. To Phoebe, they looked like fairyland castles. She hurried on, thinking of Castle Road in Greenfield.

There were few travelers on the River Road, and there were hardly any houses. But there were many fine trees. Phoebe recognized one beautiful tree as a sugar maple, and the thought of maple sugar danced into her head. Mrs. Morse, for all her meanness, had cooked good, hearty breakfasts. Phoebe's mouth watered as she remembered pancakes with maple syrup, crisp sausages, or oatmeal with thick cream.

Phoebe kept on walking, with her school satchel over her shoulder. Her shoes began to hurt her, so she took off her shoes and socks. She tucked the socks into the toes of her shoes, which she carried in one hand while holding the bunch of drooping wild flowers in the other. It was easier to walk barefoot.

Phoebe had forgotten to pack a comb, and her

curly hair was unruly. Her dress, which she had slept in, was mussed, and her hands were berry-stained. Perhaps because of her forlorn appearance, the next car stopped and the man at the wheel asked, "Can we do anything for you, little girl?"

Phoebe saw that the car was a station wagon and that there was a kind-faced woman beside the driver, as well as a flock of children in the rear seat. By this time she was longing for the offer of a ride. But she didn't quite know how to reply to the man's question, not wanting to say she was going as far away as Greenfield.

"We're headed for Brattleboro, over in Vermont, and thought you might like a lift if you're going that way," the driver went on.

Brattleboro. Phoebe remembered Ellen's postcard, and she quickly said, "Brattleboro is just where I'm going!" For hadn't Ellen written on her card, "I wish you were here"? Surely, Phoebe thought, Ellen's grandparents would help her to get in touch with her father.

"You weren't planning to *walk* all the way to Brattleboro, were you, child?" The driver's wife was speaking now. "That's more than eight miles from here. Is someone meeting you there?"

"Yes." Phoebe nodded. "I'm going to visit my best friends."

The woman looked at Phoebe searchingly, and the

children all stared at her as if she had been walking on the moon!

"Who are your friends?" asked the man.

"The Witherspoons," answered Phoebe.

"I know the name. Hop in," said the man. "There's room in the back for you with our young ones."

The back door of the car was opened for Phoebe and she climbed in, shoes, flowers, and all. The biggest girl said to her, grudgingly, "We're already crowded," which was true. In addition to five or six children, the rear of the car was filled with a lot of boxes and other things that families carry with them on a trip. Phoebe tried to make herself as small as possible, while at the same time attempting to put on her shoes and socks. Her flowers fell to the floor of the car and got stepped on by the smallest boy.

The children never stopped staring at Phoebe. They asked her, "What's your name?" and, "Why did you take off your shoes?"

Those were questions that Phoebe didn't mind answering.

Then one of the girls, who had been admiring Phoebe's locket, asked, "Are you a Gypsy?"

"No, I'm not." Phoebe tried to look indignant, but secretly she was pleased. Gypsies seemed to her romantic and exciting, because they traveled in caravans and camped in fields.

It was a long time since Phoebe had eaten her blueberry breakfast, and she was very hungry. But the family she rode with didn't stop when they came to a place that sold hamburgers and milkshakes. The children ate snacks in the car instead: corn chips, potato chips, popcorn. The smallest boy spilled half a bottle of his soft drink on Phoebe's dress.

Phoebe hoped that Ellen's grandmother wouldn't think she had spilled it.

She saw a bridge ahead, and beyond the bridge a city. The bridge led to Vermont, and the city was Brattleboro. I never guessed that Brattleboro was so big, thought Phoebe, as the station wagon nosed along its downtown streets.

The driver of the station wagon asked Phoebe, over his shoulder, "What street do your friends live on, little girl?"

"I don't know exactly," replied Phoebe.

"It will be in the phone book," said the man. He stopped at a filling station to look up the Witherspoons' address. When he came back, he said, "There's a Witherspoon on Elm Street. That's not much out of our way."

"We'll wait until your friends come to the door," his wife said to Phoebe.

But the family in the station wagon didn't have to wait. When they stopped in front of the Witherspoons' house on Elm Street, Phoebe saw Martha and Ellen on the front lawn. "There they are!" she cried.

"Are those your friends?" said the driver's wife. "Well, I can see that they are expecting you."

At the Witherspoons'

Although they said that they weren't expecting her, the Witherspoon girls didn't seem to be surprised at seeing Phoebe. "We thought you might come to Brattleboro, because your cat was here," said Ellen.

"What?" cried Phoebe. "Was Proudfoot here? When?"

"A few days ago. Maybe a week ago," said Martha. "If it wasn't your cat it looked exactly like him. We fed him, but he wouldn't stay."

Phoebe thought back. "He must have been on his way home then," she said.

Dismissing the subject of Proudfoot, Ellen said, "I'm glad you're here, Phoebe. Sit down on the grass with us."

"We're waiting for Joel to come back from the store. Grandma sent him to get some ice cream, because it's so hot," said Martha.

First, however, Phoebe knew that she had some explaining to do before she met the Witherspoon grandparents. As quickly as she could, she told Ellen and Martha how she had left Mrs. Morse and was on her way to join her father and Tom in Greenfield.

"You mean you are all alone?" said Ellen.

"What about your friends, those people whose car you were in?" asked Martha.

"They weren't my friends. They just gave me a ride," said Phoebe. "I thought, perhaps, I could spend the night here with you."

"Of course you can," said Ellen.

But Martha, who was older, said, "We'll have to ask Grandma. You've run away, Phoebe. That's what it amounts to, and most grown-ups don't approve of children running away."

"But I've got to be with Daddy and Tom," said Phoebe. Tears came to her eyes as she tried to make Martha and Ellen realize just how mean Mrs. Morse was.

They looked at her with sympathy. Ellen squeezed her hand, and Martha said, "I don't blame you for not wanting to stay with Mrs. Morse. I couldn't live with her *one day* myself. Just the same, Grandma may not approve of what you've done."

Phoebe began to dread meeting the girls' grandmother. She looked down at her dress with the stain on it from the small boy's drink. It was grape juice, she thought. She wished her appearance was neater and that she bore more resemblance to Ellen and Martha. Ellen was a squarely built little girl with blond hair and cornflower-blue eyes. Martha was blond too, but taller and slimmer. They were both wearing blue jeans and crisp flowered tops. On their feet were sandals instead of clumpy oxfords.

Phoebe asked, in a small voice, "Where is your grandmother?"

"Out back somewhere, I expect," answered Martha. "Here comes Joel. You stay with Ellen, Phoebe, while I go talk to Grandma."

Martha went to look for her grandmother as Joel came up the walk. He was a cheerful, freckle-faced boy with blue eyes like Ellen's.

On seeing Phoebe, he said right away, "Tom's cat was here. At least, we think it was Tom's cat. Did the girls tell you?"

"Yes," said Phoebe.

"Well, I've got to get inside the house with this ice cream before it all melts," said Joel. Quite obviously, he was not surprised to see Phoebe in Brattleboro. She belonged on the farm, but the farm was not very many miles away.

Grandmother Witherspoon came out to speak to Phoebe. She was young-looking and brisk, not a bit the way Phoebe thought grandmothers ought to look. She had on a pink pants suit and had beauty-parlor hair. After inviting Phoebe to spend the night, she asked, "What happened to your dress?"

"A little boy spilled some grape juice on it," said Phoebe.

"That's too bad," said Grandmother Witherspoon. "Now tell me, Phoebe Tucker, does your housekeeper know where you are?"

Phoebe was silent, wondering just what to say.

"Speak up," said Grandmother Witherspoon.

"She doesn't know," said Phoebe.

"We'll have to tell her. But first let's go and have some ice cream," said Grandmother Witherspoon.

Holding tight to Ellen's hand, Phoebe went inside the house.

The children were all seated in the spick-and-span kitchen when Grandmother Witherspoon said to Joel, "Run and fetch your grandpa, please. He's out in the backyard garden and doesn't know we've got company."

"Grandpa's hard of hearing," Martha explained to Phoebe.

When Grandfather Witherspoon came into the kitchen, Ellen introduced Phoebe to him, saying, "This is my best friend, Grandpa."

"How do you do?" said the old man, holding out his hand. Phoebe thought he looked rather stern, like his son at the farm.

"Phoebe is going to spend the night here," said Ellen.

"Indeed," said Grandfather Witherspoon, helping himself to some ice cream.

After the ice-cream party was over, Martha and

Ellen took Phoebe upstairs to their room. "You're to sleep here with us. Grandpa's going to put up a cot for you," said Martha.

Phoebe thought the room was pretty. The twin beds were painted white like her own bed at the farm. But she felt anxious, because she was afraid that Grandmother Witherspoon would try to make her go back to Mrs. Morse. She asked Martha and Ellen, "Does your grandmother know my father?"

"Grandma's heard of him, but she says he's a busy man and oughtn't to be bothered," said Martha. "Sh-h. Here comes Grandma."

Grandmother Witherspoon came into the girls' room to say that she had just phoned Mrs. Morse and that Grandpa was going to drive Phoebe back to the farm in the morning.

Phoebe began to cry. "I wanted to phone *Daddy*," she said.

"I tried to call your father, Phoebe. I got his phone number from my son. But I was unable to reach him," said Grandmother Witherspoon.

Phoebe was in despair. She was afraid to go back to Mrs. Morse now. She was sure some awful punishment lay in store for her. Martha and Ellen's faces were as long as Phoebe's.

But their grandmother said, "You are overtired, Phoebe, and what you need is a good rest. If Ellen will lend you one of her dresses, I'll wash out yours. I

use vinegar for stubborn stains like fruit juice." She patted Phoebe's shoulder.

After their grandmother had left the room, Ellen and Martha both put their arms around Phoebe. "We're on your side," said Ellen.

"Yes. We'll try to think of some way to save you from going back to that old Mrs. Morse," said Martha.

They were true friends, thought Phoebe. More than that, they were *brave* friends. Being on Phoebe's side when their grandparents were not took courage.

Neither of the Witherspoon girls knew how they were going to help Phoebe, but with Phoebe's consent they decided to ask Joel's advice. He was sure to be on Phoebe's side, just as they were, and he was a boy who had good ideas and who knew how to keep a secret.

The Bus Station

Phoebe had a hot, sudsy bath that afternoon, and then she put on a dress loaned to her by Ellen. She looked so fresh and pretty that all of the Witherspoons paid her compliments, all except Grandpa.

He asked her, "Do you know what little girls deserve who run away?"

"N-no, sir," said Phoebe.

"Well, in my day they got a spanking," declared Grandpa Witherspoon.

The three young Witherspoons, pretending that they hadn't heard, asked Phoebe to come out in the garden with them. There, sure of not being overheard, they told her of their plan. Early in the morning, before their grandparents were awake, Joel would conduct Phoebe to the bus station.

The idea of Phoebe's taking a bus to Greenfield was Joel's. He asked her, "How much money do you have?"

"Eight dollars," said Phoebe.

"That ought to be more than enough," said Joel. "You're under twelve, so you'll only have to pay half fare."

"Are you sure there's a bus that goes to Greenfield?" asked Phoebe.

"Positively, cross-my-heart sure," said Joel. "That's a big place."

Phoebe's heart lifted. Soon, very soon, she would see her father and Tom. No one had answered the phone when Grandmother Witherspoon called their number, but Phoebe knew that her father was seldom at home in the daytime and Tom had a part-time job.

They'll be there sooner or later, and they'll be glad to see me, thought Phoebe.

She enjoyed the supper Grandmother Witherspoon cooked and didn't mind being sent to bed right afterward. Martha and Ellen went upstairs with her. Their grandmother called after them, "Mind now. No staying up late and talking. Phoebe's going to get an early start in the morning, and I want to see her eat a good breakfast first."

Phoebe couldn't help feeling a bit guilty, because she knew she wouldn't be having breakfast at the Witherspoons'. She would be at the bus station or on a bus. Martha and Ellen were used to getting up early on the farm, and they promised to waken Phoebe as soon as it was light.

"What about Joel?" Phoebe asked.

"Oh, he has an alarm clock, and he sleeps downstairs in the den, where no one else can hear it," said Martha.

"Not even your grandmother?" asked Phoebe.

Grandpa Witherspoon might be hard of hearing, but Phoebe didn't think there was anything wrong with Grandmother Witherspoon's ears.

"I don't see how Grandma can hear it, because *I* can't," said Martha.

Phoebe felt so nervous and at the same time so excited that she had a hard time getting to sleep in her cot. She wished that it was already morning. Her dress was dry; it hung neatly over the back of a chair, along with her underclothes. Her shoes were placed side-by-side underneath the chair. She had on her own pajamas. I won't need more than a minute to get dressed and packed, thought Phoebe.

She didn't remember falling asleep. . . . All at once, however, she saw that the sky outside the window was light, and she knew that morning had come. Ellen was standing beside her bed. "Are you awake, Phoebe? It's time for you to get up," whispered Ellen.

Phoebe put her finger to her lips; she didn't dare to say a word. Quickly she dressed herself and got ready to leave. With her satchel over her shoulder and her shoes in her hand, she tiptoed down the stairs.

Joel was waiting for her. He lifted the night chain from the front door, and they went out together. Joel didn't need to tell Phoebe to hurry, because she felt like running all the way to the bus station. However, once they were out of sight of the house, Phoebe stopped in order to put on her shoes.

Joel stood by while she tied the laces. "Be quick,

Phoebe. Grandpa is an early riser," he said.

The bus station was five blocks away. When they finally reached it, Phoebe exclaimed, "Safe at last!"

But Joel was not so sure. He looked back to see if Grandpa Witherspoon had followed them.

Phoebe wasn't at all familiar with bus stations. The only kind of bus she had ever ridden on was her school bus. But Joel knew his way around the station in Brattleboro. He headed for the ticket counter to ask when the next bus would leave for Greenfield. He hadn't been able to call up from the house for fear that his grandmother would hear him.

Even though it was early, there were other people ahead of Joel at the ticket counter. He took his place at the end of the line and told Phoebe to stand behind him. "Have your money ready. I'll buy your ticket for you," he said. Joel acted toward Phoebe just like an older brother.

Phoebe stood close behind Joel and looked in her satchel for her money.

When Joel's turn came, he asked the ticket seller, "Is there a bus leaving soon for Greenfield, Massachusetts?"

"You've just missed one," the man replied. "The next bus for Greenfield doesn't go out till eight."

Joel repeated this information to Phoebe. It was only six now, as they could see by a clock on the wall behind the counter. "You're going to have a two-hour wait, Phoebe, and I can't stay with you," said Joel.

"I've got to get back to the house before Grandma and Grandpa wake up."

Phoebe knew Joel was right. But she hated to be left alone in the bus station. "Can you buy my ticket now?" she asked.

"If you'll hand me the money," said Joel.

But before Phoebe could do so, he gave her a little push and said, "Quick, Phoebe. Hide!" Startled, she looked past him at a man who was entering the bus station. The man was Grandpa Witherspoon, and he looked very, very angry.

There was hardly time for Phoebe to hide, but she darted away from the ticket counter in a flash. Dodging behind first one grown-up person, then another, she wished with all her might that she could be invisible.

She passed a drinking fountain. Could she hide behind it? No. *Anyone* could see me there, thought Phoebe. A telephone booth would be better. There were three booths in a row, and she slipped inside the first one. She pulled the door shut behind her and crouched down on the floor. Her heart was beating so fast that it sounded to her like a clock. People passed by. Phoebe heard their footsteps. But nobody opened the door. No one knew she was hiding in that telephone booth.

Phoebe still had all of her money, because there hadn't been time for Joel to buy her ticket to Greenfield.

On Toward Greenfield

Phoebe felt cramped in the telephone booth, but she didn't dare to stand up, for fear that her head would show through the glass part of the door. She wished she could try to phone her father. But even if she stood up to reach the phone, she wouldn't have known how to call him. Phoebe had never used a pay phone.

She wondered what had happened to Joel. Had his grandfather seen him and asked him about her? Poor Joel, thought Phoebe. He had been really good to her!

Just when Phoebe had decided that she could stay no longer in such a stuffy place, someone rapped on the door of the telephone booth and a face peered in through the glass. It wasn't Grandpa Witherspoon's face. So Phoebe got to her feet, opened the door, and asked, "Do you want to use this phone?"

A rather grumpy lady said, "Yes, I do. I don't know what game you think you are playing, little girl."

Phoebe walked past her. The bus station was more

crowded than it had been when she and Joel first arrived. Phoebe could see no sign of either Grandpa Witherspoon or Joel, but she was afraid that they might still be there. Though Joel might have scooted home, the chances were that Grandpa Witherspoon was still looking for her.

The clock above the ticket counter showed that the time was nearly seven. Phoebe wondered if she dared to walk up and buy her bus ticket. While she was trying to make up her mind she spied a man at the counter who looked like Grandpa Witherspoon! She turned and fled, her only thought being to hide again.

There were other children in the bus station, some with their parents and others in a group who looked to Phoebe as if they were going to a camp. Each child was carrying a piece of luggage, and three or four had tennis rackets. Phoebe was thinking of hiding among these children when she noticed, straight ahead, a door with the word *ladies* on it. Grandpa would not dare follow her in there! Phoebe thought.

She went inside, and the door swung shut behind her. Once more Phoebe felt safe.

Several women were in the rest room. No one spoke to Phoebe until a young woman who was powdering her nose in front of a mirror asked, "Are you all by yourself?"

Phoebe thought it best not to answer her. She edged away, murmuring, "I've got to catch my bus."

Unfortunately, it wasn't nearly eight yet. Phoebe opened the door a crack and peeped out. She was afraid to go back to the ticket counter to buy her ticket.

All at once Phoebe made up her mind not to take a bus, but to start walking toward Greenfield as she had the day before. Perhaps another family might offer her a ride! In any case, she was eager to leave the dangerous bus station.

She walked out of the rest room behind a stout woman who made a sort of shield for her, and in a few minutes she was on a street that was busy with people going to work. Phoebe walked quickly, hoping that no one would stop her and start asking questions.

The only town Phoebe knew well was Linton. It was a small town, but it was big enough for the schoolchildren to be taught how to cross streets safely. Brattleboro was about ten times larger than Linton, and naturally there was a lot more traffic. But Phoebe watched the lights change from red to green and knew when it was safe to cross. She read all the traffic signs, watching out for the ones that said *South* or *Mass*. Greenfield was south of Brattleboro, and it was in Massachusetts. She wondered, as she had often wondered before, just how Proudfoot had traveled. He had secret paths and secret shortcuts near the farm but how had he managed in a city?

Phoebe glanced back over her shoulder. The

thought kept jumping into her mind that Grandpa Witherspoon was following her. She felt hunted, the way a wild, small animal must feel. I'm like a possum or a coon or a scared little rabbit, thought Phoebe. She wished she would come soon to the end of Brattleboro!

After Phoebe had walked ten or twelve long blocks she saw a farm truck parked at a filling station. The truck was loaded with vegetables: big sacks of potatoes and baskets filled with green beans, beets, and onions. Phoebe was used to seeing farm trucks just like this one, and she looked at it admiringly.

"A pretty sight, isn't it?"

Phoebe jumped.

A jolly-looking man in overalls was pumping gas into the truck and had noticed Phoebe's admiring glance. "I'm really proud of my vegetables," he said. "I sell all the way from Brattleboro to Greenfield."

At that, Phoebe said, "I'm going to Greenfield."

"You don't mean that you're *walking* to Greenfield," said the man.

Phoebe confessed that was what she intended to do. "My father and my brother are already there," she said. After a moment she added, "Daddy gave me some money. I could go on a bus, but I don't want to wait for a bus."

"Why is that? Waiting for a bus is better than walking," said the man.

Not wanting to argue, Phoebe walked on.

"Wait a minute!" the man called after her. "What's your father's address in Greenfield?"

Phoebe turned back. "It's 10 Castle Road," she told the man.

"I know where that is. If you've told me the truth, I can give you a lift there," he said.

"I *did* tell you the truth," said Phoebe.

He must have believed her, because he said to climb into his truck while he went inside the filling station to pay for his gas. Soon they were on their way, heading toward the south, toward the state of Massachusetts and the city of Greenfield. Phoebe was glad when they passed the last house in Brattleboro.

Having had no breakfast, Phoebe was hungry. Otherwise, she was happy. She thought that trucks were more fun to ride in than cars, because the rider sat up higher in them and could see more of the world. The world Phoebe saw this morning looked new and sparkling to her. There were red-and-white cows in a green field, white sheep on a hillside, and a family of young pigs in a pen beside a barn.

"Those pigs are cute," Phoebe remarked.

The man beside her laughed. He said he had never thought of pigs as being cute. "But a cat now. My wife has a cute cat," he said.

Phoebe thought again of Proudfoot.

"I saw a cat — a black cat — the other day in Brattleboro," the man went on. "He was a smart cat! He was waiting for the traffic light to change, just like a man."

That was Proudfoot, thought Phoebe. Her heart swelled with pride. She asked the man, "Did the cat you saw have topaz eyes?"

"I couldn't tell you. I wasn't that close," he replied.

Phoebe was certain, however, that the cat he had seen was Proudfoot.

The truck was equipped with a radio. The man said, "Let's have some music," and he turned the radio on.

Just then Phoebe saw a sign: *Welcome to Massachusetts.* She cried out in excitement, "We're in Massachusetts now!"

"I know that," said the man. "Be quiet, will you?"

Instead of music a news report was coming over the radio, and he was listening to it.

Phoebe listened too. She heard a voice say, "The missing girl was last seen at the bus station in Brattleboro." A description of the missing girl followed: she was nine years old, had curly brown hair, and wore a brown-and-white checked dress.

That's me, thought Phoebe.

The man beside her looked alarmed.

"She may have been kidnapped," said the voice coming over the radio.

Abruptly, the driver pulled his truck to a stop just off the highway and told Phoebe to get out. "I'm not a kidnapper, and I don't want to be fined for taking you across a state border," he explained.

Phoebe clutched her satchel tightly. She felt too startled to say a thing, and she climbed down from the truck.

"There's a farmhouse down the road a piece where you can stop," said the man. "They'll be good to you there. Good luck." And he drove off.

Phoebe stared after the truck as it grew smaller in the distance. Here she was, on the way to Greenfield, but that city seemed to her as far away as ever.

Gypsies or Hippies

If Phoebe hadn't been so hungry she might not have stopped at the farmhouse, but kept on walking along the grass that edged the highway. She was very hungry, though. The sun was high up in the sky, and Phoebe guessed that the time was nearly noon. If the people in the farmhouse gave her some lunch, she could pay for it, because she had spent none of the dollars her father had given her.

Phoebe saw the house. It was on her side of the road, set back on a rise of land that was not quite a hill. From the highway, the farm, with its barn and its silo, looked like a toy farm. But as Phoebe approached the house a large dog rushed at her, and he was by no means a toy dog.

He was barking furiously.

Phoebe backed away. Although she was fond of most animals Phoebe was afraid of huge barking dogs. This one looked to her rather like a wolf. She backed away one more step.

Then a woman's voice called out, "Stop that, Rover! You ought to be ashamed, barking at a poor little girl."

The woman was standing in the doorway of the

farmhouse. She had gray hair, and she wore a blue apron over her print dress. At her words the dog slunk toward the house with his tail between his legs. At least that barking dog knows how to mind, thought Phoebe.

"Come in, you poor little thing," the woman said to Phoebe. "Rover won't hurt you. What are you doing here all by yourself?"

Phoebe felt confidence in the farm woman, who had a kind face and a gentle manner. In a rush, she told her who she was and where she was going, and the woman didn't send her away or scold her for leaving Mrs. Morse. She said to Phoebe, "You must be hungry. Let me give you something to eat, and we'll talk about what to do afterward."

A few minutes later Phoebe was seated in the farm kitchen, while the woman, whose name was Mrs. Baxter, put good things to eat on the table. There were slices of cold ham, warmed-over biscuits, and a wedge of apple pie.

"Do you like milk?" asked Mrs. Baxter.

"I love it," said Phoebe. "Aren't you going to eat something too?"

"No, I'm going to wait for my husband," replied Mrs. Baxter. "He doesn't usually come in till after one o'clock."

While Phoebe ate, Mrs. Baxter told her about her family. She had a married daughter and two grown sons, the younger of whom hadn't settled down yet.

"Grant's a good boy, but I just don't care for some of his friends," Mrs. Baxter said.

Rover was barking again.

"Someone's here. You can go on with your lunch," Mrs. Baxter said to Phoebe, and she went to the door. Phoebe had eaten enough, so she left the kitchen and peeped out from behind her.

A car had stopped in front of the house, and Rover was jumping around it, barking madly. There were two young men in the front seat and two girls in the back. Phoebe didn't think that any of them looked much older than Tom. The car, an old one, was decorated with stickers and painted-on flowers.

Rover kept barking, and the boy at the wheel tooted his horn. No one could speak above the racket until Mrs. Baxter cried, "Rover, be quiet! And Grant, you leave that horn alone!"

In the hush that followed, Phoebe heard her say, "So you're back again, Grant. Are you here to stay this time?"

"No, Mom," he replied, getting out of the car. "I just stopped by to see if you could lend me some money. I'm on my way to Greenfield, to look into a job I heard of."

Phoebe took hold of Mrs. Baxter's hand to remind her that she was there, and Mrs. Baxter, looking somewhat doubtful, asked her, "Do you want to go with him?"

"Oh, yes!" said Phoebe.

"Very well. That may be the best way," said Mrs. Baxter. "You can trust Grant. He'll get you to your father in Greenfield. But stay close to him. Pay no attention to the hippies."

Phoebe thought she said Gypsies. Were those girls and the other young man Gypsies? Phoebe looked at them again before she went to get her satchel. The clothes they wore were rather wild, and so was their hair. "I expect they *are* Gypsies," Phoebe said to herself.

Mrs. Baxter wouldn't let Phoebe pay for her lunch. "No, child, keep your money. I enjoyed your company," she said. "Remember what I told you."

"I will," Phoebe promised.

"Thanks, Mom," said Grant, as his mother handed him some money. He agreed to take charge of Phoebe and to deliver her safely to her father. Meanwhile, his friends waited silently in the car.

I'm *really* going to Greenfield now, thought Phoebe, as Grant headed his car toward the highway. She sat between the two young girls, both of whom wore as many strings of beads as if they were Gypsies. Phoebe learned that their names were Annabel and Lynn. They asked her what hers was, but they decided to call her Grasshopper instead of Phoebe. "You look like a little brown grasshopper in that brown dress," said Lynn.

"Grasshopper is a good name for her," said the boy who sat beside Grant.

They don't talk like Gypsies, thought Phoebe.

She began to feel uneasy. The old car couldn't go fast, but Grant was making it go as fast as possible. "There's another old car. Watch me race it!" he said to his friends, and he forced his car past the other, missing it by inches.

Mrs. Baxter had said to Phoebe, "You can trust Grant." Phoebe wondered if she knew what a crazy driver he was. "Stop!" she cried, when he began to race a bus.

Grant didn't listen to Phoebe. He charged after the bus, which in no time outdistanced him.

Afterward Grant drove less wildly. He sang as he drove, and his friends chimed in. They all sounded as happy as could be. Phoebe didn't know the words of the song they were singing, but the tune was one that she and Tom had often heard.

Suddenly Grant stopped his car in front of a roadside eating place. "Who's hungry? I can treat anyone to a lunch," he said.

His friends all said they were hungry. But Phoebe had already eaten. "I had lunch at your mother's," she said to Grant.

"Good," he replied. "You can stay in the car. See that nobody steals it."

He was joking, thought Phoebe. She watched the four young people get out of the car and go inside the restaurant. No one would think of stealing an old, jolty car like Grant's. She tucked her feet up under her and made herself comfortable.

While waiting for the others to return, Phoebe thought about all the things that had happened since she left the farm. Sleeping in the Haunted House was scary, but Proudfoot was with her then. The Witherspoons saw a black cat, she thought, and the man in the truck saw a black cat. If those black cats were Proudfoot — and Phoebe felt sure they were — he knew how to get around in a city. She wondered if he had ever jumped in cars or on trucks in order to get rides!

The young people came back to the car looking happier than ever. "Make room for us, Grasshopper," said the girl named Annabel. "We're going to a festival now."

"What?" cried Phoebe. "Aren't we going to Greenfield?"

"Sure we are," said Grant. "But we're going to this festival first, Grasshopper."

"Come on, let's go hopping," said the other boy.

Grant started the car, and they went off down the highway, everyone singing except Phoebe. She wondered what they meant by a "festival." Was it some kind of party?

Phoebe felt too worried to sing, for she knew by this time that Grant was in no hurry to get to Greenfield. She felt still more worried when, a mile or two past the restaurant, he turned off the highway onto an unpaved road. "Grant's taking some secret way, like Proudfoot," Phoebe told herself. But that thought didn't comfort her.

After passing through a countryside that reminded Phoebe of home, Grant drove his car off the road and into an open field. Phoebe saw that many other cars were already parked there. Some of them were old, like Grant's, but some were as new as her father's. There were vans too. Phoebe thought they looked something like Gypsies' wagons.

"Is this where the festival's going to be?" asked Phoebe.

Nobody seemed to hear her. Grant and his companions were too busy greeting other boys and girls they knew.

Phoebe got out of the car. She didn't see any other nine-year-olds, though no one in that field looked really grown up. The festival is going to be a picnic, thought Phoebe, for she saw some tablecloths and blankets spread out on the grass. Among the young people were a number who strummed guitars and sang. Others played tunes on harmonicas. When a few got to their feet and began to dance, Phoebe stepped out of their way. She was startled when someone suddenly caught hold of her and said, "Come on, little one, let's be merry!"

A Black Cat Appears

Phoebe never had a good look at her partner, who whirled her around so fast that her feet left the ground. She was thinking, This is fun, when she saw her school satchel lying on the ground. She didn't want to lose it, with all her money inside it, so she cried out, "Let go of me!"

Her partner gave her one more spin before he let her go. By then a young girl had picked up the satchel and was rummaging through it. Phoebe said, "That's mine. Give it back to me!"

The girl, who was neither Annabel nor Lynn, said, "All right. There's nothing much in it." She let Phoebe take the satchel. It was precious to Phoebe, for besides the money it contained the few belongings she had brought with her from the farm. Keeping a tight grip on it, she moved away from the dancers and sat down on the grass.

Phoebe didn't see Grant anywhere, and she wondered when she was going to get to Greenfield. She was too worried to be hungry, but when the afternoon light faded and food was passed around, she accepted a piece of cheese and an apple. There was nothing to drink that Phoebe liked — only beer and sour-smelling wine — so she went without. They made her think of a rhyme she had learned from one of her schoolmates:

Whisky and rum
Make you dumb.

All at once, while everyone was eating, Phoebe became aware that she had lost her gold locket. Had someone taken it? Or had it slipped from her neck when she was being whirled around by her dancing partner? Phoebe didn't know, but she kept searching for it until the sun had set and the sky was sprinkled with stars. The moon had not yet risen.

Although Phoebe couldn't find Grant, she saw his car at the edge of the field where he had parked it. Sooner or later, she thought, he would return to the car. She decided to get inside it and wait.

Phoebe was half asleep when she saw a black shape leap through the car's open window. She thought she must be dreaming. "Proudfoot, is that you?" she asked, in wonderment, touching the silky coat of a large cat.

The cat didn't purr in reply, but looked at Phoebe with yellow, or topaz, eyes that shone in the dark.

Phoebe thought, The cat that stopped at the Witherspoons' might have been some other cat, and the cat the man in the truck saw might have been another, but *this* cat is certainly Proudfoot! He must have decided not to go back to the farm after all, but to help me get to Greenfield. "Did you come here in a car, just like me?" she asked him.

The cat began to purr with Proudfoot's same old rumbling purr.

Unseen by anyone, Phoebe and the black cat left the car and stole off into the friendly shadows. Phoebe knew that Proudfoot had his own secret paths. The fact that this black cat seemed to know exactly where he was going convinced her that he was indeed Proudfoot.

"I *know* he's Proudfoot," she said to herself, keeping close behind him.

They crossed one empty field, and then another, while the moon rose and shone down on them. The cat often looked back, in Proudfoot's old way, as if to make sure that Phoebe was still there.

Of course I'm still here, thought Phoebe. She had a lot more confidence in Proudfoot than in Grant. But she was getting very tired of walking. She felt her dress tear as she climbed over a fence, which the cat had slipped under with no difficulty.

After what seemed to Phoebe like a long, long time she saw some far-off lights illuminating the sky, and she guessed that they were approaching a city. Was it Greenfield? she wondered. Hoping that it was, she squared her shoulders and stepped more briskly after her guide. Before long they reached a highway strung with chains of lights. To Phoebe's surprise, the cat stopped in front of a roadside restaurant that had the words *Open All Night* on its sign.

"Are you hungry?" she asked the cat, when he sat down in front of the door.

Phoebe wasn't hungry, but she felt like resting, and she thought she would like something hot to drink. She pushed open the door and went inside the restaurant. The cat, tail up, strolled in with her.

"Can I bring you something to eat?" asked the woman.

"No, thank you. But I'd like some hot cocoa," said Phoebe.

A tired-looking woman, who stood behind the counter, asked Phoebe, "Where's the rest of your family, dear?" Then, before Phoebe had a chance to reply, she noticed the cat and said, "I'm sorry, but pets aren't allowed in here."

Phoebe turned to leave.

"Wait," said a man, getting up from one of the tables. "It's okay with me if the cat stays." He whispered something to the woman, who looked at Phoebe closely.

"There wasn't anything about a cat in the report," said the woman.

Phoebe was glad when she was invited to sit down

at a table and when her companion was allowed to stay.

"What's your name?" the woman asked.

"Phoebe Tucker," she replied willingly, "and this is my brother's cat."

"And how about some scrambled eggs?"

"That will be fine," said Phoebe. She remembered that Proudfoot liked a taste of scrambled eggs now and then.

While the woman was attending to Phoebe's order, the man went to a telephone behind the counter. Two couples who were eating at a table kept on talking to each other.

Phoebe wasn't paying attention to anyone in the restaurant. She had laid her school satchel on the table in front of her and was looking inside it for money to pay for her order. But her eight dollars were gone! Phoebe turned quite pale.

"What's the matter?" asked the woman, bringing her the scrambled eggs and cocoa.

"I haven't any money," said Phoebe, and she began to cry.

"Never mind. Just go ahead and eat," said the woman. "We're expecting someone, almost any minute now, who'll pay for your order."

Phoebe was frightened. She had no idea who was coming. Could it be Grandpa Witherspoon or even Mrs. Morse? She stood up, not knowing whether to run or to stay.

The cat was looking at the scrambled eggs expectantly. Phoebe didn't want them. She put the plate in front of him, and then she heard the sound of a siren coming closer and closer.

A policeman walked into the restaurant. He glanced once at Phoebe, then said to the man who had telephoned, "This is the little girl all right."

Phoebe was surprised, but she wasn't afraid anymore. She had watched enough television shows with Tom to know that policemen were good. They helped people who had been wronged and punished the ones who had been bad — just like Robin Hood.

The policeman came over to her and said, "So you're here, Phoebe Tucker."

"Yes, sir," she said. "I've been trying to get to Greenfield."

"This is Greenfield. We are just within the city limits. Your father is on his way here now," said the policeman.

Phoebe was so excited that she never knew when, or exactly how, the black cat disappeared. Suddenly she saw that his chair and his plate were empty. Then her father and Tom arrived.

Safe in Greenfield

Phoebe's father lifted her up in his arms and held her close while he spoke with the police officer and the man who had telephoned. Phoebe put her arms around her father's neck and snuggled her head against his shoulder. She didn't listen to all that was being said, but she learned that her father had been searching for her ever since he had heard the radio report of a missing girl named Phoebe Tucker.

Phoebe looked at Tom, who stood beside his father's elbow and who hadn't a chance to say a word. "Proudfoot was here," she told him.

Ignoring that statement, Tom asked her, "Why did you run away?"

"Don't ask Phoebe questions now, Tom," said his father. "She's exhausted. Wait until we've taken her home."

Home means Greenfield, not the farm, thought Phoebe. She didn't want to think about Mrs. Morse. "But Proudfoot *was* here," Phoebe said aloud.

"My rascally black cat! He couldn't have been." Tom was listening now.

"Oh, yes, there was a cat here." Several voices spoke at once.

"Proudfoot found me way off in a field where there was a big party going on, and I followed him back to the highway," said Phoebe.

"You're crazy," said her brother. "Proudfoot wouldn't be rambling around down here. I bet he's in our old barn right now, catching mice!"

No one, however, either then or afterward, could make Phoebe believe that the cat who had jumped inside Grant's car wasn't Proudfoot.

Dr. Tucker wouldn't let go of Phoebe. He carried her out to his car and put her in the front seat, where she sat secure and safe between him and Tom. No questions were asked of her, and soon she fell asleep with her head against her brother's arm. She didn't open her eyes until they reached the house that her father had rented on Castle Road. There was no castle on that street, but the Tuckers' house was a pretty one.

"Here I am at last!" said Phoebe.

"You've probably had a lot of adventures since you left the farm," said Tom. He spoke rather enviously.

Phoebe yawned. She was safe in Greenfield, where she wanted to be, and she didn't expect to have any more adventures.

Her father had a serious talk with Phoebe the next morning. After she had told him about her overnight stay at the Witherspoons' and the truck driver and the festival, he took her on his knee and said, "Now, Phoebe, I want you to tell me why you ran away from the farm. Mrs. Morse phoned me, but not until after I'd heard you were lost on the radio. She said she was too upset to call before and that there was no reason for you to leave her."

"That's not true, Daddy. I had *lots* of reasons." Phoebe proceeded to tell him about some of the things that had made her very unhappy. His arms tightened around her when she said, "Mrs. Morse wanted to make me think that you didn't love me."

"I love you with all my heart, Phoebe. I was coming for you in two weeks. Didn't Mrs. Morse tell you that?" said her father.

"No, Daddy. Mrs. Morse didn't tell me anything. She just talked to her old witchy friends," said Phoebe. "They came every week, and I went to my room to keep out of their way."

"Phoebe, honey," said her father. "You must not make things up. I don't understand about the *witchy* friends."

"There were three of them." Phoebe rattled off their names and added, "They didn't come to the farm until you'd gone away. Mrs. Morse made me get the sitting room ready for them. It was always Phoebe do this, and Phoebe do that."

Her father looked so angry that Phoebe would have

felt shaken if she hadn't known he was angry with Mrs. Morse, not her. "Mrs. Morse and I are going to have a showdown," he said. "I have to look after my patients now, Phoebe, but Tom is waiting to show you around the neighborhood." For Tom's tutoring was over with, and his part-time job, which was helping in a supermarket, was only in the afternoon.

Phoebe was left in Tom's care when their father, on his first free day, drove up to the farm to confront Mrs. Morse. Two letters arrived for Phoebe on that same day, both of them postmarked *Linton*, *N. H.* While Phoebe studied the envelopes, Tom stood waiting to hear what was inside them.

The first letter Phoebe read was from Ellen.

Dear Phoebe,

How are you? We came home yesterday. And your cat is here. We may have seen a different one at Grandma's.

We miss you.

Love,
Ellen Witherspoon

The other letter, from Martha, was longer.

Dear Phoebe,

Grandma and Grandpa were very upset when they found you had gone, and they gave Joel a big scolding for taking you to the bus station. But now they say you were right all along. They don't like Mrs. Morse anymore, because Papa told them that she's acting funny. She has three friends staying with her, and they are real creepy. You are lucky you got to your father and Tom. But we miss you. Good luck.

Your friend,
Martha

P.S. Your father phoned Grandma to say you were all right.

Phoebe handed Tom her two letters. After he had read Ellen's, he said, "I *knew* Proudfoot was at the farm. He's a country cat, and he doesn't like cities."

"I don't think he really likes Mrs. Morse either," said Phoebe. What Proudfoot liked was the barn and catching mice and following his own, secret paths. . . .

"As to Martha's letter," said Tom, breaking in on Phoebe's thoughts, "I'm not sorry if everyone's turned against Mrs. Morse. She was mean to you. But even so, Phoebe, you've no idea how *scared* Dad was when he heard you had run away. Something bad could have happened to you."

"Something bad did happen," said Phoebe. "I lost my gold locket, with Mother's picture in it, and someone stole all my money."

Phoebe never returned to the farm. When her

father came back from his showdown with Mrs. Morse, he told Tom and Phoebe that he was going to sell the farmhouse as soon as he could find a buyer.

"What did Mrs. Morse say to that?" asked Phoebe, who couldn't believe that anyone, not even her father, could dislodge their housekeeper.

"Mrs. Morse had *nothing* to say. I paid her well while she lied to me and tried to keep my family apart. She has to move in with her friends — those women you called witchy — whether she likes it or not," said Dr. Tucker.

"I called them witchy because they looked like witches," said Phoebe. "And I think, Daddy, that Mrs. Morse *might* be a witch too."

Her father rumpled her hair and said, "You've read too many stories. No, Mrs. Morse is not a witch, but a selfish, mean, deceitful woman. Let's forget about her now, Phoebe. I'm going to take you downtown and buy you some pretty new clothes!"